Helen Orme taught as a Special Needs Co-ordinator in a large comprehensive school. At the last count she had written around 40 books, many for reluctant readers.

Helen runs writing workshops for children and courses for teachers in both primary and secondary schools.

Taken for a Ride

Helen Orme

Taken for a Ride

by Helen Orme
Illustrated by Cathy Brett
Cover by Anna Torborg

Published by Ransom Publishing Ltd.
Rose Cottage, Howe Hill, Watlington, Oxon. OX49 5HB
www.ransom.co.uk

ISBN 978 184167 596 1

First published in 2007

A CIP catalogue record of this book is available from the British Library.

Meet the Sisters ...

Siti and her friends are really close. So close she calls them her Sisters. They've been mates for ever, and most of the time they are closer than her real family.

Siti is the leader – the one who always knows what to do – but Kelly, Lu, Donna and Rachel have their own lives to lead as well.

Still, there's no one you can talk to, no one you can rely on, like your best mates. Right?

For Amy Taylor

1

Riding lessons – ugh!

Lu met up with Donna on the way to school.

"Guess what they've done for my birthday," she said.

"What?" Donna was a bit jealous of all the things Lu got.

"Riding lessons – ugh!"

"You lucky thing!" Now Donna was really jealous.

"I'd love riding lessons. I asked if I could, but all I got was the usual 'We can't afford it.'"

"You could have mine any day. I hate horses, they're smelly and stupid!"

Donna knew differently, but she wasn't going to argue.

At school Lu told the Sisters about her birthday present.

They tried to think of ways to help.

"Can't you just tell your mum?" asked Siti.

"I tried," said Lu. "You know what she's like."

"What can I do? I've got to get out of it. Help me!"

2

Break a leg

"What about your dad?"

"No. He's worse. He just tells me how lucky I am."

"I know," said Rachel. "Why don't you fall off – on purpose – and break a leg?"

"Bit drastic," said Kelly. "It might stop the lessons, but it would stop a lot of other things too!"

"You need a stand-in, like they have in the movies," said Rachel.

"Maybe that's not so dumb," said Siti. "Get someone else to do it instead."

She looked at Donna, who had kept very quiet. "How about you? You love horses."

"Yeah, go on," said Kelly. "Pretend to be Lu!"

"What do you think?" said Siti, looking at Donna.

"Yeah, I'll give it a go."

"Problem!" said Lu.

"What?" They all looked at her.

"My parents. Mum's going to take me next weekend. I can't swap after I've started and we can't swap before. So it's just not going to work."

"You could always try breaking an arm," said Rachel, as they went off to their tutor group.

3

We can do it!

Lu tried again, but mum just wouldn't take any notice.

"It's not fair!" she told Siti. "She doesn't listen to anything I say."

"Typical! – my mum never listens either."

"But I hate horses! Come on Siti – think of something."

But not even Siti could think of a plan that would work.

Saturday came. Lu sulked all through breakfast, but mum didn't notice.

The phone rang.

"That was Gramps," said mum. "Gran was up a ladder, painting, and fell off. They've gone to the hospital. They want me to go. I'll call dad and get him to take you to the riding school."

She pulled a face. "He won't be pleased, he's so busy..."

Dad was in I.T. He had an office near the town centre.

Lu thought quickly. “No, you’re all right – I’ll go by myself. I’ve got my phone. I’ll keep in touch.”

“I’ll book a cab.”

“Don’t panic mum, just get off to the hospital. I’ll go by bus. I can get Siti to come with me.”

Mum wasn’t thinking about Lu. She was worrying about Gran.

“O.K., whatever you want. Call me later.”

Mum rushed off.

Lu rang Siti.

“We can do it – Donna can go instead!”

She told Siti about her Gran. Siti took control.

"You ring Donna – I'll get the others sorted. We'll all come with you."

4

No one will ever know

Lu's mum had rung. Gran had a broken arm and she'd hit her head too, so the hospital wanted her to stay.

"Everyone's here," said Lu. "They'll come with me and stay while I have my lesson. Talk to you later."

Siti checked the bus times and worked out which bus to catch. Lu was much happier

now she knew she wasn't going to have to get on a smelly old horse.

Donna was really excited.

"Are you sure it's going to be O.K.? What'll happen if they find out I'm not you?"

"Don't worry," said Siti, "No one will ever know."

"What am I going to wear?"

"No probs," said Lu. "I've got all the stuff and you're just my size. Even the boots will fit."

They met Mrs Samways the owner of the stables. She took Donna off. The Sisters went to sit on some benches nearby. Soon Mrs Samways came back with Donna and a horse. Donna was dressed in Lu's riding gear.

"You look great," called Rachel.

"Shut up," said Siti. "You'll get us thrown out."

Mrs Samways gave Donna a boost up onto the horse. It looked quite hard. She showed Donna how to hold the reins, then took hold of another long rein herself. She patted the horse on his rump and he started to walk slowly round.

Donna had a big grin on her face.

She was happy.

5

Feeling guilty

The weeks went by – and things were going well. Lu spent Saturday afternoons in town with one or more of her friends. Often they went to the shopping centre. It was a good place to hang out.

Sometimes Lu felt a bit guilty. Especially when her mum and dad asked how she was getting on. It was easy to answer. She knew all about it.

Donna was having a fantastic time. She loved the horses, she loved everything! She wouldn't shut up about it.

"They're going to have an open day," she said. "To show off the stables and the horses. I'm in the display."

"We'll all come and watch," said Siti.

They all went to the open day.

"Don't forget we've got to call Donna 'Lu'," said Siti.

Mrs Samways was giving out prizes.

"And now the prize for the best beginner," she said. "Lu Clarke. She's one of the best riders we've ever had."

Siti, Lu, Kelly and Rachel clapped and clapped like mad.

"You were great!"

"Fantastic!"

"Well done!"

Mrs Samways came over.

"Hello," she said. "Your friend is going to be a star."

She looked at Donna. "I need to talk to your parents, Lu," she said. "I want to train you. You will need more lessons and more time at the stables. I'm sure we can fix up something. Ask your mum to call me."

She smiled, and walked off.

Donna was grinning all over her face. Lu had gone white.

"Oh no!" she said. "What am I going to tell them? They'll kill me!"

6

Telling the truth

"You'll just have to tell them the truth," said Siti.

Donna felt really bad. "I'm sorry," she kept saying. "It's all my fault. I just loved it so much I couldn't help myself."

"It's not your fault! Mum and dad should have listened to me in the first place."

"But now you'll get into trouble, so will I, and I'll never be able to go riding again."

"I know," said Siti. "We'll go and see Mrs Samways."

"I suppose," agreed Lu.

Next day was Monday so they went after school.

They decided that only Siti, Lu and Donna would go.

Mrs Samways looked pleased.

"What did your mum and dad say?" she asked.

Donna burst into tears.

"Come indoors and tell me all about it," said Mrs Samways.

Mrs Samways was really nice, but she said she couldn't let it go on.

"I'm sorry, my dears," she said. "I just can't do it."

She turned to Lu. "If I was your mum, I'd want the truth."

Then she looked at Donna. "But I don't want you to have to give up. Is there any chance ...?"

But Donna didn't let her finish. "No way," she said. "We just can't afford it."

7

We should have listened . . .

Lu opened the front door. Mum came out into the hall.

"I want a word with you, young lady."

"What have I done now?"

Her mother gave her the local paper.

There was a report about the open day. There was a big picture of Donna with a caption saying 'Lu Clarke, the best rider we've ever had.'

"Explain, please," said mum.

Lu told her mum everything; how she hated horses and how much Donna loved it.

"Couldn't you go on paying for Donna's lessons?" she asked. "She's really, really good."

"So I see," said mum. "But that's not really our problem, is it?"

"What are you going to do?"

"I don't know. I'll need to talk to your dad. Go upstairs and stay there."

Lu went.

She heard her dad come home. She heard talking.

The phone rang.

The talk went on again.

What were they going to do to her?

There was a knock at the door.

"Lu, come downstairs," called her dad.

She went down. Donna was there with her mum and dad. They were smiling. Even mum didn't look so cross.

"I told them," said Donna. "They rang Mrs Samways, and she's rung your dad."

Lu looked at her dad.

"You're right," he said. "We should have listened to you."

"But don't ever do anything like this again," put in mum.

"I won't, I'm so sorry," said Lu. "But what about Donna? Why are you looking so pleased? I thought you'd be really sad."

"It's all sorted," said Donna. "Mrs Samways has fixed it. I've got a job at the stables. I can work one evening every week and she'll go on giving me lessons. Isn't it great!"

"And you can go too," said dad, looking at Lu. "Your punishment is to go and be a stable girl for a term. Mrs Samways has a really big shovel for mucking out!"

"Oh well," said Lu. "Anything's better than riding."